POLLYANNA

Eleanor H. Porter

adapted by
Marion Leighton

Illustrations by
Gual

BARONET BOOKS, New York, New York

BARONET BOOKS is a trademark of Waldman Publishing Corp., New York, N.Y.

Printed in the United States of America

Table of Contents

About The Author
Eleanor H. Porter

Eleanor Hodgman Porter was born in New Hampshire in 1868. She didn't spend much time in school during her childhood, because her family believed that being outdoors would make her stronger!

She loved music. After completing her studies at the New England Conservatory of Music in Boston, she became a choir leader, singer and teacher.

When she was 24 years old, Eleanor married John Lyman Porter. They traveled to Tennessee and later settled in New York. Eleanor began to publish books—first short stories and then many novels for both adults and children. She sometimes used the pen name of Eleanor Stuart.

Pollyanna, written in 1913, was Eleanor's most successful book and was widely read in many countries around the world. Eleanor wrote several other books about this little "glad" girl. In 1920, the year that Eleanor Porter died, the first film version of *Pollyanna* was produced.

There have been many other movie and television versions of this very successful, beloved novel.

“Put the Dishes Down and Pay Attention!”

Chapter 1

Miss Polly

Miss Polly Harrington was in a great hurry. It was very unusual for Miss Polly to rush, so Nancy knew right away that something was afoot.

"Nancy, listen to me!" snapped Miss Polly to the servant girl. "Put the dishes down and pay attention!"

Nancy always experienced a combination of fear and anger when Miss Polly spoke to her. She never seemed able to please her demanding mistress and was afraid of losing her job. But she certainly didn't like to be scolded all the time.

"When you finish your kitchen duties, you may clean the little room in the attic and make up the cot," said Miss Polly. My niece, Miss Pollyanna Whittier, will sleep in that room. She is eleven years old and is coming to live with me."

"It will be so nice to have a little girl here!" said Nancy, already feeling sorry for the child.

"I would hardly call it nice," replied Miss Polly. "But I will do my duty and take care of her."

"Of course, ma'am. I just thought that a little girl would, uh, brighten up the house."

Miss Polly glared at Nancy.

"But don't you want your sister's child?" Nancy persisted.

"Well, really, Nancy, I hardly look forward to taking care of a child that my sister was silly enough to bring into a world that's already too full of children. But there's no more time for talk. My niece will soon be here. Be sure to

“Don’t You Want Your Sister’s Child?”

clean in all the corners of the attic."

Miss Polly retired to her bedroom and glanced again at the letter from the faraway Western town: "Dear Madam," it began. "I am sorry to inform you that the Reverend John Whittier died two weeks ago. He left a daughter, Pollyanna. Since he was the husband of your dead sister, I hope that for your sister's sake you will take care of the little girl and bring her up. A couple from our church will travel with Pollyanna on the train to your town in Vermont. Please let me know immediately if these plans are okay." The letter was signed "Jeremiah O. White."

"What an unpleasant surprise!" muttered Miss Polly for the umpteenth time. "And what a silly name—Pollyanna!"

Miss Polly was 40 years old and quite alone in the world. Her large house on top of a hill seemed empty without children or friends. Miss Polly spent most of her time reading or sewing. She hardly ever went into town except

"What an Unpleasant Surprise!"

for meetings of the Ladies Aid, a group of women from the church who did volunteer work and gave money to good causes.

But the last thing Miss Polly wanted was the company of a little girl who would probably bang doors, drop silverware, and generally make a mess of the house! The mistress of the Harrington estate was not looking forward to this new period in her life.

The Last Thing Miss Polly Wanted

"Stickin' That Child Up Here!"

Chapter 2

A Talk With Old Tom

"Imagine havin' such a big house with so many rooms to choose from and stickin' that poor child up here!" Nancy muttered as she finished cleaning the little attic room.

Nancy's family didn't have much money, but at least the children—there were six brothers and sisters altogether—didn't have to sleep in hot little rooms without any pictures or toys.

When she finished cleaning, Nancy went out into the yard. Old Tom, the gardener, was on his knees pulling out the weeds.

"You'll never guess what happened!" Nancy greeted him. "Miss Polly's little niece is comin' to live here!"

"That's a good joke!" said Tom. "Next you'll tell me the moon is made of green cheese!"

"But it's true about the girl. Miss Polly told me so herself!" said Nancy.

Tom turned serious. "You know," he said softly, "I'll bet it's Miss Jenny's little girl! Glory be! I never thought I'd live to see this!"

Tears came to his eyes.

"Who was Miss Jenny?"

"She was an angel! But the old master and missus sure didn't like that minister she married. She went away with him and never came back. We later found out that all her babies died except one. That must be the little girl who's coming here. But I wonder what Miss Polly will do with the child."

"*I* wonder what the *child* will do with Miss Polly!" replied Nancy.

Tears Came to His Eyes.

"I guess you're not too fond of Miss Polly."

"Well, I guess *nobody* is!"

The old man laughed.

"Some people were at one time. I guess you never heard about Miss Polly's romance."

"Romance—*her?* Now you're the one who's telling a joke!"

"I'm telling the truth! And the man still lives right in this town too!"

"Who is he?"

"I can't tell you that. Wouldn't be right." Tom was a loyal servant who had worked for the Harrington family since he was a very young man.

"Miss Polly and a *sweetheart!"* said Nancy.

"Well, if you'd known Miss Polly like I did, maybe you'd believe it. She used to be right handsome. And she still could be too if she'd just let her hair down loose and wear a bonnet with flowers in it and put on a pretty dress and a lace shawl. You know, Nancy, she's not very old."

"Romance—*Her*?"

"Well, I sure wouldn't put up with her except that I need this job to provide for my family. But some day I'll get so mad that I'll just quit!" Nancy declared.

"I'll Just Quit!"

The Little Attic Room

Chapter 3

Pollyanna Arrives

Miss Polly checked out the little attic room, with its small, neatly made bed, two straight-backed chairs, a chest of drawers, a wash-stand, and a table. The summer heat was unbearable. But worse for Miss Polly was the fly in the room. Frowning, she killed the insect.

"Nancy, I found a fly in Miss Pollyanna's room," she announced angrily when she went downstairs. "I ordered some screens, but I expect you to make sure that the windows remain closed until they are delivered. Oh, and by the way, my niece will arrive tomorrow,

June 25th. I want you to meet her at the train station. The telegram I received says she has light hair and will wear a red-checked gingham dress and a straw hat. That should be enough for you to recognize her."

"But . . ." Nancy started to say.

"I know what you're thinking, Nancy. I shall not go to meet Pollyanna. I have made up my mind. That is all."

Timothy, Old Tom's son, drove Nancy to the train station with the horse and carriage.

"Let's just hope the kid doesn't slam doors or drop silverware," Timothy laughed. "That would drive Miss Polly crazy!"

Nancy spotted the little girl immediately. She was standing alone on the platform looking all around. Nancy approached her nervously.

"Are you Miss . . . Pollyanna?" she asked softly. The child didn't answer but reached out and hugged Nancy so tightly that she could barely catch her breath.

Timothy Drove Nancy to the Station.

"Oh, I'm so glad, *glad*, GLAD to see you! Of course I'm Pollyanna, and I'm so glad you came to meet me. I knew you would!" She let go of Nancy briefly and jumped up and down, all the while eyeing her from head to toe. "I just couldn't wait to see what you look like! And I'm glad you look like you do!"

Timothy approached and asked Pollyanna for her luggage.

"Oh, I have a brand new trunk," bubbled the child. "The Ladies' Aid from the church bought it for me. Don't you think it was nice of them, 'specially because they wanted the carpet so much. I'll bet they could have bought a whole aisle of red carpet for the cost of that trunk!"

Pollyanna talked continuously during the ride home.

"What a lovely place!" she said when they arrived at the Harrington house. "I knew it would be pretty. Father told me. . . ."

Nancy noticed that her chin was shaking and there were tears in her eyes. But Pollyanna re-

"Of Course I'm Pollyanna!"

covered quickly and lifted her head bravely.

"Father remembered everything. Oh, and I should have explained about this red gingham dress and why I'm not wearing black since father died. The problem is there weren't any black things in the last Ladies' Aid barrel—only a black velvet thing that the deacon's wife said wasn't any good for a little girl. And, besides, it was worn out and had some spots on it. The Ladies' Aid wanted to buy me a black dress and hat, but some people said the money should go for the church's red carpet instead. Anyhow, I guess it's true that children don't look good in black . . ."

"I'm sure it's all right," Nancy broke in.

"Well, I'm glad you feel that way. Anyway, it would be much harder to feel glad in black."

"Glad?" asked Nancy sharply.

"Well, yes. Father's gone to heaven to be with mother and the rest of the family. He said I must be glad, but it's been hard because they all have each other but I was all alone. That's why

"Glad?" Asked Nancy Sharply.

I'm so glad that now I have you, Aunt Polly!"

Nancy was horrified.

"Oh, you've made a mistake, honey. I'm not your Aunt Polly. I'm just Nancy, and we're not anything alike. Not at all!"

"But who *are* you? asked Pollyanna fearfully. "You don't look at all like a Ladies' Aid person either. And *is* there an Aunt Polly?"

"I'm no Ladies' Aider. I'm just the hired girl."

"So she *is* alive. I'm really glad! In fact, I'm glad she didn't come to meet me because now I have you and her too!"

Pollyanna stared at the house. "Is my Aunt Polly very rich, Nancy?"

"Yes, miss."

"I'm so glad! It must be lovely to have lots of money. The only rich people I knew were the Whites. They have carpets in every room and ice cream sundaes. Does Aunt Polly have ice cream sundaes?"

"No, miss," said Nancy. "I reckon she don't like ice cream because I've never found any in

"Is My Aunt Polly Very Rich?"

her kitchen."

"Really? But does Aunt Polly have carpets?"

"Oh, yes, lots of carpets."

"In every room?"

"Well . . . almost every room," replied Nancy, thinking about Pollyanna's bare little attic room.

"Oh, I'm so glad!" said the little girl. "I love carpets. All we had were two rugs that came in the church barrel, and they had ink stains on them. Oh, but Mrs. White also had pictures in her house. Pictures of roses and little girls and a kitten and some lambs and a lion. The lion and lambs weren't together, you know. The Bible says that someday they will be, but they aren't yet—that is, Mrs. White's aren't. But I *do* love pictures!"

As Timothy unloaded Pollyanna's trunk and carried it into the house, Nancy thought to herself, "I won't think about leavin' here after all! That poor little child will need someone to protect her from Miss Polly, and it'll be me!"

"That Poor Child Will Need Someone!"

Holding Out Her Hand

Chapter 4

A Room In The Attic

Miss Polly was reading when Nancy and the little girl arrived. She did not get up from her chair.

"How do you do, Pollyanna?" she said, holding out her hand dutifully. But the child darted across the room and flung herself onto her startled aunt's lap.

"Oh, Aunt Polly, Aunt Polly! I am *so, so glad* that you let me come to live with you! It's so lovely to have you and Nancy after having just the Ladies' Aid!"

"I imagine so," said Miss Polly with a frown

as she tried to remove the little girl's clinging arms from her neck. "Now please stand up, Pollyanna, and let me see what you look like."

Pollyanna laughed nervously as her aunt's eyes inspected her.

"I guess I'm not very pretty because of my freckles. Oh, and I ought to explain about the red gingham dress and the worn-out black velvet thing with the spots on it. Father said . . ."

"Never mind what your father said," Miss Polly interrupted. "I suppose you have a trunk?"

"Oh, yes indeed, Aunt Polly. I have a lovely trunk that the Ladies' Aid gave me. I don't have many clothes. But I *do* have Father's books. Mrs. White said I ought to keep those . . ."

"Listen to me, Pollyanna," said Miss Polly. "Let me make it clear from the start that I don't care to have you talk about your father! Now let us go up to your room."

The child grew silent, and tears welled up in

"Let Me See What You Look Like."

her eyes.

"I guess I should be glad that she doesn't want to hear about father," Pollyanna said to herself. "Maybe it will be easier for me if I don't talk about him. I miss him so terribly!"

As they went upstairs, Pollyanna looked at all the rooms with their beautiful furniture, lacy curtains, and deep soft carpets.

"What a lovely house, Aunt Polly! You must be glad to be so rich!"

Her aunt turned around sharply.

"Pollyanna! I'm surprised at you! It would be sinful to be proud of the gifts that the Lord gave me!"

Miss Polly was relieved now that she had arranged for her niece to live in the plain and sensible attic room. Besides keeping her away from valuable things that she might soil or break, she would break her pride.

Pollyanna's imagination wandered as she walked through the big house. She tried to guess which of the wonderful and interesting

Rooms With Beautiful Furniture

rooms might be her very own. But soon they passed the lovely sights and climbed another flight of stairs to a hot little space where the roof almost met the floor. Suitcases and boxes were stored there, along with oversized bags holding Miss Polly's winter clothes. Miss Polly opened a door on the right and turned to her niece.

"Here is your room, Pollyanna. Do you have the key for your trunk?"

Pollyanna nodded.

"When I ask you a question, please answer out loud instead of just moving your head."

"Yes, Aunt Polly."

"I think you have everything that you need here, Pollyanna," said her aunt, pointing toward the towels hanging neatly on the rack and the water in the pitcher. "I will send Nancy up to help you unpack your trunk! Supper will be served promptly at six o'clock every evening."

After Miss Polly left, Pollyanna stared un-

The Roof Almost Met the Floor.

happily at the hard floor, the empty walls, and the bare window. Then she fell to her knees by the bed and sobbed her heart out. Nancy found her there a few minutes later and wrapped her arms around her.

"I was fearin' you might feel this way, Miss Pollyanna."

"Oh, Nancy," cried the child, "it's just so hard for me to understand that God and the angels needed my father more than I did . . ."

"They did *not*, either!" Nancy thought to herself.

"There, now, give me the key and I'll try to unpack your things," she said out loud.

"There aren't too many of them," Pollyanna said tearfully.

"Well, then, we'll unpack them that much more quickly!"

"I guess I can be glad about that, don't you think?" said Pollyanna, smiling suddenly.

Nancy didn't answer but continued to unpack the books and the patched clothes.

"It's Just So Hard for Me."

"I'm sure this will be a very nice room," continued Pollyanna. And I'm really glad that there isn't a mirror, because now I won't be able to see my freckles!"

Suddenly Pollyanna clapped her hands with joy.

"Oh, look, Nancy! Look out the window at the beautiful trees and houses and the church steeple and the river shining like silver. Now I won't need any pictures *inside* to look at! I'm really glad now that Aunt Polly gave me this room!"

Nancy, horrified, burst into tears.

"What's wrong, Nancy?" asked Pollyanna, hugging her new friend.

"Why, you're a little angel straight from heaven, and that woman . . . Oh, drat, there's her bell calling me!"

Nancy left the room and raced downstairs to her mistress.

The hot sun was burning into Pollyanna's room. The little girl raised the window sashes.

Pollyanna Clapped Her Hands with Joy.

Flies buzzed in, but she hardly noticed. She leaned out and saw a large tree with long branches that seemed to invite her to play. Pollyanna stepped onto the window ledge and, from there, grabbed the nearest branch and swung from limb to limb. She had always loved to climb trees.

It was quite far from the lowest branch to the ground, but she made it, landing on hands and knees in the soft grass. She breathed the fresh air happily.

Pollyanna found herself at the back of the house. An old man was working in the garden. Beyond the garden was a path leading through an open field and up a hill to a pine tree standing alone next to a big rock. She raced toward the path.

The dinner bell rang at exactly six o'clock. When Pollyanna failed to appear, Miss Polly frowned, tapped the floor with her foot, and finally sat down at the table alone. Nancy went into the hall to see whether the child was com-

Pollyanna Grabbed the Nearest Branch.

ing down the stairs.

"My niece is late, Nancy, but do not call her. I told her what time supper is served. She must learn to be prompt or suffer the consequences. When she comes down, you may give her bread and milk in the kitchen."

As soon as dinner was over, Nancy crept up the back steps to the attic room, muttering to herself:

"Bread and milk indeed! Pollyanna hasn't eaten all day. She must be starved. And the poor little lamb's been cryin' her eyes out."

Nancy opened the door to the attic room and called Pollyanna. There was no answer. The child was not there! Nancy looked in the closet, under the bed, and even inside the trunk. In panic, she flew downstairs and out to the garden.

"Mr. Tom, Mr. Tom! The child is gone! Vanished! She's surely gone straight up to heaven and is eatin' angel food. Bread and milk indeed!"

“Bread and Milk”

Tom smiled and pointed ahead.

"Well, she sure tried to get as close to heaven as she could! There she is, on top of that rock yonder!"

“As Close to Heaven as She Could!”

"You Sure Scared Me!"

Chapter 5

The Game Of "Glad"

Nancy was breathless when she reached Pollyanna.

"You sure scared me!" she said.

"Father also got scared when I disappeared. But he finally understood that I always found my way back home," Pollyanna explained.

"But nobody even saw you leave the house," said Nancy. "You must've gone straight up the roof!"

"No, not up. I went down. Right down the tree by my window!"

"Well, for heaven's sake!" gasped Nancy. "I'd

like to know what your aunt would say to that!"

"Well, how about if you ask her and find out?"

"Mercy, no! *No!*"

It was getting dark, and Pollyanna held tight to Nancy's hand.

"I guess I'm glad you got scared, because you came after me. Otherwise I would have to have come back by myself."

"Poor little lamb! And you missed supper too! I fear that you'll have to have bread and milk in the kitchen with me."

"It's all right, Nancy. Don't worry about that. I'm glad!"

"Glad? Why?"

"Well, because I like bread and milk, and I really want to eat supper with you so we can talk together."

"You sure seem glad about everything," Nancy remarked.

"Well, that's the name of the game," said

"I'm Glad!"

Pollyanna with a laugh.

"The *game*?"

"Yes, the 'just being glad' game."

"What in the world are you talking about, Pollyanna?"

"It's a real game, Nancy. Father taught it to me."

"But what *is* it?" asked Nancy.

"Well, we began the game when some crutches came in a barrel of things that people gave to the church," she began.

"Crutches?"

"Yes. You see, I wanted a doll, and Father told the Ladies' Aid. But when the barrel came, the ladies said there weren't any dolls but there were some little crutches that maybe a child could use someday."

"Well, that doesn't sound much like a game," Nancy remarked.

"But it *was*," insisted Pollyanna. "The game was to find something to be glad about in everything—no matter what it was."

"The 'Just Being Glad' Game," Said Pollyanna.

"Well, that sounds strange to me," said Nancy, somewhat annoyed. "How can you possibly be glad to get crutches when you wanted a doll!"

"Well, I couldn't see it either, at first," Pollyanna admitted. "Father had to explain it to me."

"Well, how about if *you* explain it to *me*?" snapped Nancy.

"Why, it's simple!" Pollyanna said, clapping her hands. "Just be glad you don't *need* the crutches!"

"Well, if that's not the weirdest thing I ever did hear!"

"But it *isn't* weird! It's lovely!" insisted Pollyanna. "And the harder it is to feel glad, the more fun the game is. Except sometimes it's almost *too* hard—like when Father went to heaven and I didn't have anybody left but the Ladies' Aid."

"Or when you get an ugly little room in the attic," Nancy added.

"Be Glad You Don't *Need* the Crutches!"

"That *was* hard at first," Pollyanna admitted. "But then I got to thinking how I hate to see my freckles in a mirror and how I don't really need pictures on the walls because beautiful things are outside my window. So I knew I could still find things to be glad about. Trouble is, there's nobody to play the game with now. You don't suppose Aunt Polly would play, do you?"

"Her?" Nancy grunted. "Of course not. But wait, Miss Pollyanna. I can't say I'll play the game real well, but I *will* play it with you. Yes, I will!"

"Thank you, Nancy!" said Pollyanna, giving her a bear hug.

Downstairs, Miss Polly was in her chair reading as usual. "Did you have your supper, Pollyanna?" she asked, keeping her eyes fixed on her book.

"Yes, Aunt Polly."

"I'm sorry that I had to make you eat bread and milk in the kitchen the very first day you were here."

"Did You Have Your Supper?"

"But I'm really glad about it, Aunt Polly. I like bread and milk, and Nancy too. Don't feel sorry."

Miss Polly stared at her niece. A strange feeling came over her.

"Time for bed, Pollyanna. Tomorrow we must plan your time and also decide what clothes to buy for you. Nancy will give you a candle to take to your room. Be careful how you handle it. Be sure to be downstairs for breakfast at exactly 7:30."

Pollyanna gave her aunt a hug. "I've had such a lovely time here so far. Your house is beautiful! And I know I'm going to like living with you. Good night, Aunt Polly!" she said cheerfully.

"What an amazing child!" muttered Miss Polly to herself after Pollyanna left the room. "She's glad I punished her and she's going to love living with me!"

Upstairs, lonely little Pollyanna sobbed into her pillow.

Pollyanna Gave Her Aunt a Hug.

"I know, Father among the angels, that I'm not playing the game now—*not one bit!* But I bet even *you* wouldn't find anything glad about being alone in this dark room. If only I could be near Nancy or Aunt Polly—or even a Ladies' Aider!"

“Alone in This Dark Room”

"I'm Glad Just to Be Alive!"

Chapter 6

Schedules, Duties and Punishments

Pollyanna awoke early the next morning. The sky was pure blue, and she ran to the window to talk to the chirping birds. Seeing her aunt in the garden, she dressed quickly and ran to join her.

"Oh, Aunt Polly, I reckon I'm glad just to be alive on this beautiful morning!" She flung her arms around Miss Polly's neck.

"Is this the way you usually say good morning?" asked Miss Polly, pulling away from the embrace.

"Only when I love people a whole lot!" said the little girl. "I got to thinking that you really are my aunt—not just a Ladies' Aider. And I was so glad that I had to hug you!"

"That will do for this morning!" said Miss Polly, walking away.

Pollyanna lingered in the garden.

Mr. Tom looked at her tearfully. "You look so much like your mother, little miss! I've been workin' here ever since she was a little girl like you."

"Really? You knew my mother? Please tell me all about her!" Pollyanna plopped down on the ground next to the gardener. But suddenly a bell rang and Nancy ran out to fetch Pollyanna.

"That bell means a meal's bein' served, Miss Pollyanna," she said breathlessly. "And you need to run fast as you can when you hear it. If you don't, it'll be hard for you or me to find anything to be glad about!"

Miss Polly was seated at the breakfast table

“So Much Like Your Mother!”

and frowning.

"Nancy!" she said sternly, "where did those flies come from?"

"Oh, I reckon they're my flies," Pollyanna chimed in.

"*Yours?"* Miss Polly screamed.

But where did they come from?"

"From outside, of course, Aunt Polly. More of them are in my room."

Miss Polly turned to Nancy with a look of horror on her face.

"Go at once to Miss Pollyanna's room and close the windows. Then get the fly squatter and check every room in the house!"

She turned to her niece. "I did my duty and ordered screens for those windows. But you have forgotten *your* duty."

"My duty?"

"Yes, of course. I know that your room is hot, but you mustn't open the windows until the screens arrive. Flies are not only dirty and noisy but also very dangerous to your health!

"I Reckon They're My Flies."

They have many germs. After breakfast, I will give you a booklet on this subject."

"Oh, thank you, Aunt Polly! I love to read. And I promise not to open the windows again."

Pollyanna was reading when Miss Polly entered her room.

"Oh, I never knew so many interesting things about flies . . ." the little girl began.

"That'll do, Pollyanna," her aunt replied sternly. "Go to your closet now and bring me your things."

"I'm afraid you won't like them," said Pollyanna, biting her lip. "Even the Ladies' Aid said they were awful. And, of course, they'd have been black if it wasn't for the carpet for the church. Did you ever have a church barrel, Aunt Polly?"

Her aunt stared in disbelief.

"Oh, of course you didn't. Rich people don't need those things. But I forgot how rich you were, being up here in this room, you know . . . Anyway, barrels were also the hard-

“I’m Afraid You Won’t Like Them.”

est thing to play the game on. Father and I . . ."

She stopped quickly, remembering that Aunt Polly had told her not to talk about her father. Her aunt changed the subject quickly.

"I suppose you have gone to school, Pollyanna?"

"Oh, yes, Aunt Polly."

"Very well. You will enter school here in the fall. I suppose it's my duty to listen to you read aloud each day for half an hour."

"Oh, I love to read, Aunt Polly. But if you don't want to listen, I'd be very glad just to read to myself!"

"I'm sure that's true, Pollyanna. Have you studied music?"

"I played piano at church, but I like other people's music best."

"Well, it's still my duty to teach you some basic things about music. You know how to sew, I hope?"

"I Suppose You Have Gone to School?"

"Oh, yes, ma'am. The Ladies' Aid taught me."

"And cooking?"

"They taught me that, too. I can make chocolate and fig cake."

"Chocolate and fig cake, indeed!" snorted Miss Polly, making some notes on a pad of paper.

"Here's your schedule, Pollyanna. Each morning after breakfast, you will make your room neat. Then, from nine o'clock until nine-thirty you will read out loud to me. After reading, you will sew with me—except for Wednesdays and Saturdays, when Nancy will teach you how to cook. Afternoons will be for your music."

"But, Aunt Polly, you haven't left time for me just to—to live!"

"What on earth do you mean, child? As if you aren't living all the time!"

"Of course, I'm breathing all the time—even when I'm asleep. But that isn't living! Living

"Here's Your Schedule."

is playing outdoors, climbing hills, talking to Mr. Tom and Nancy, and exploring . . ."

Miss Polly sighed and frowned.

"Of course, you will be allowed a proper amount of playtime. But it seems to me that if I'm willing to do my duty to give you proper care and instruction, you should be willing to do *your* duty by making sure that this care and instruction aren't wasted."

Turning to leave, she added, "Timothy will drive us into town at one o'clock this afternoon. I would not be doing my duty if I let my niece wear those clothes that you brought. We shall buy new and proper ones."

"Thank you, Aunt Polly, but, please, isn't there *any* way that you can be glad about that duty stuff?"

"Don't be disrespectful, Pollyanna!" her aunt scolded.

"The only thing left to do," Pollyanna thought to herself, "is to be glad when the duty is done!"

"You Will Be Allowed Proper Playtime."

At exactly one o'clock, they set out to buy material to sew Pollyanna's new clothes. The salespeople fell in love with the cheerful and talkative child. After shopping and eating dinner, Pollyanna played the "glad" game with Nancy.

"I just hate my name," said Nancy. "All my brothers and sisters have such pretty names . . . Florabella, Estelle . . ."

"But I *love* the name Nancy, just because it's you!" said Pollyanna. Anyway, you should be glad that your name isn't Hepzibah!"

"Hepzibah? What kind of name is that?"

"That's Mrs. White's name. Her husband calls her Hep!"

Nancy burst out laughing. "Maybe I should be glad after all."

Soon it was Pollyanna's bedtime. She undressed, folded her clothes neatly, said her prayers, blew out her candle, and climbed into bed. She lay sleepless for hours in the heat and finally opened the door and walked to the win-

Material for Pollyanna's New Clothes

dow outside her room. A full moon lit up the attic.

Below the window was the tin roof of Miss Polly's sun parlor. The garment bags with winter clothes hung on hooks near the window. Pollyanna chose two large bags, opened the window far enough to push them down onto the roof, and climbed out. She made a mattress and pillow with the bags and curled up to sleep.

Inside the house, Miss Polly was pale with fright. She phoned Tom.

"Please come right away with a ladder and lantern. Someone is on the roof of my sun parlor!"

Tom and Timothy climbed a ladder, peered over the edge of the roof, and chuckled when they saw the girl, but Miss Polly was not amused.

"Pollyanna! What does this mean?" she shrieked in horror.

"It's all right, Aunt Polly. It's just that my

Tom and Timothy Climbed a Ladder.

room was *so* hot. But I closed the window behind me so the flies couldn't get in the house!"

"Pollyanna, until the screens come, you will sleep in my bed with me. It is my duty to know where you are always!"

"Oh, thank you, Aunt Polly! It will be so nice to stay in your room! Now I won't be so lonely!"

Soon Pollyanna was sleeping peacefully on her aunt's soft sheets. A pink satin beadspread covered her. It matched the curtains on Miss Polly's windows.

A grateful Pollyanna snuggled in.

Soon Pollyanna Was Sleeping Peacefully.

"What an Extraordinary Child!"

Chapter 7

A Visit To Mrs. Snow

"What an extraordinary child!" Miss Polly Harrington exclaimed daily as she watched her niece perform her routines. She was relieved that she had allowed Pollyanna a period of free time from two until six every afternoon. Not only did the little girl need time to "live," but her aunt had to recover from the whirlwind of planned activities—and the endless chatter!

Pollyanna always wanted to do errands so that she could walk around the neighborhood and explore her new surroundings. One day,

Miss Polly asked her to carry a jar of calf's-foot jelly to Mrs. Snow, a member of the church who could not get out of bed. Miss Polly felt duty-bound to deliver something to Mrs. Snow every week.

"Let me just warn you," Nancy said, "you're not goin' to be glad about this errand—not one bit! I've been to that woman's house many times. When you bring jelly to Mrs. Snow, she wants chicken, and when you bring chicken, she's hankerin' for lamb broth. There's just no pleasin' her!"

"Sort of like tryin' to please Miss Polly!" Nancy thought to herself.

Milly, Mrs. Snow's daughter, led Pollyanna to her mother's room. Mrs. Snow was propped up in bed.

"How do you do, Mrs. Snow? I am Pollyanna Whittier, and my aunt, Miss Polly Harrington, asked me to bring you some calf's-foot jelly."

"Dear me! Jelly?" the woman groaned. I was

Milly Led Pollyanna to Her Mother's Room.

hoping it would be lamb's broth."

"Oh! I thought it was chicken you wanted when folks brought you jelly."

"What did you say?" asked Mrs. Snow. "Oh, never mind! I didn't sleep a wink last night!"

"But people lose so much time sleeping. Don't you think so?" asked Pollyanna. "Sleeping takes time away from living!"

"Well, you really are amazing!" exclaimed Mrs. Snow. "Open the curtain so I can look at you!"

Pollyanna went to the window and pulled back the curtain. "Oh, now you'll see my freckles! But I'm glad you wanted to see me, because now I can see you too. They didn't tell me you were so pretty!"

"Me pretty?"

"Yes! You have big, dark eyes and nice black curly hair."

Mrs. Snow was only forty years old, but she had been confined to bed for fifteen years. The doctors said she would never be able to walk

“I Thought It Was Chicken You Wanted.”

again. Pollyanna picked up a small mirror and moved toward the bed. Then she stopped.

"Why don't you let me fix your hair before I let you see yourself?" she said. "May I, please?"

"Well, I guess so," said Mrs. Snow, who was more amazed at every moment with her young visitor.

"Oh, thank you! I love to fix people's hair," said Pollyanna, reaching for a comb. She arranged the curls and then placed a pink flower in Mrs. Snow's hair.

"Now, take a look!" she smiled, handing Mrs. Snow the mirror.

"Humph! I must say that I like red flowers better than pink ones, but they all fade by nightfall anyhow."

"But you should be glad they fade, 'cause then we can get more. But your hair *does* look lovely!"

"Hmm, maybe. But it will get messed up again when I toss back and forth on my pillow."

“I Love to Fix People’s Hair.”

"Well, I'm sort of glad about that, because then I can fix it up again. I just love black hair!"

"Well, it's hard to love anything at all when you have to lie in bed everyday from morning to night!"

Pollyanna looked at her.

"I guess it *would* be hard to be glad about things in that case."

"You bet!" snapped Mrs. Snow. "Just try and think of anything I could possibly be glad about!"

Suddenly, Pollyanna sprang to her feet and clapped her hands. Mrs. Snow stared at her in disbelief.

"Oh, goody! This is going to be a hard one! But I'll think about it all the way home, I promise, and maybe next time I come I can tell you! Goodbye for now! I've had a lovely visit with you!"

"Well, I never!" exclaimed Mrs. Snow.

"Mother, the curtain is up!" exclaimed Milly,

"The Curtain Is Up!"

entering the room after Pollyanna left. "And you have a flower in your hair!"

"At least she didn't see me with the mirror!" thought Mrs. Snow.

The next week, Pollyanna visited Mrs. Snow for the second time. Her bedroom was dark again, but she called out to her young visitor, "I remember you! But I wish you had come yesterday. I really wanted to see you yesterday!"

"Well, I'm glad that it's only one day later than yesterday!" Pollyanna laughed. "Now let me see how you look!" she said, opening the curtains. "Oh, you haven't fixed up your hair. But I'm glad, because maybe you'll let me do it. But right now I want you to see what's in this big basket that I brought you." Pollyanna set the basket on the table by the bed.

Mrs. Snow frowned.

"What do you want most?" asked Pollyanna.

Mrs. Snow hesitated. She wasn't used to getting what she wanted.

"Well, of course, there's lamb broth . . ."

She Wasn't Used to Getting What She Wanted.

"I've got some!" chuckled Pollyanna.

"But that's what I *didn't* want," sighed Mrs. Snow. "I really wanted chicken."

"Well, I've got that too!" Pollyanna exclaimed.

"You have *both?"*

"Yes—and calf's-foot jelly too!" smiled Pollyanna. "I told Nancy I wanted to be sure you got *something* that you wanted, so we fixed all three! I hope you don't mind that there's just a little bit of each thing." She placed three little bowls on the table. "And how do you feel today?" she asked.

"Quite poorly. The lady next door was playing the piano, and I've been thrashing around in this bed all morning trying to sleep!"

"Well, I'm glad that you can thrash around. Mrs. White, one of my Ladies' Aiders, was so sick once that she couldn't even move! She told me afterward that she probably would've gone crazy if it hadn't been for Mr. White's sister's ears!"

"A Little Bit of Each Thing"

"What?"

"Oh, you see, the sister was deaf and she came to help take care of Mrs. White. And whenever the neighbor played the piano, Mrs. White was so glad she could hear it instead of being deaf! You see, I had taught her how to play the game."

"Game?" gasped Mrs. Snow.

"There! I almost forgot that I told you I would think of something to be glad about even though you have to lie in bed all day. And I must admit that it was very hard. But the game is more fun when it's hard! Anyway, I finally thought of something!"

"And what might that be?"

"Well, I thought how glad you could be that other folks weren't always sick in bed like you are!"

"Well, really!" Mrs. Snow grunted.

Pollyanna certainly had not meant to say anything that might upset her new companion. She smiled at her.

“Game?” Gasped Mrs. Snow.

"I have to hurry home now," said Pollyanna. "I'm sorry there isn't time to fix your hair, Mrs. Snow. But at least I'm glad that I have legs to hurry with!"

Mrs. Snow didn't answer. But when Milly came into the room, she saw tears in her mother's eyes.

Tears in Her Mother's Eyes

"I'm Glad Your Days Are Happy."

Chapter 8

Switching Rooms

July passed very quickly. Pollyanna often hugged her aunt—to Miss Polly's dismay—and told her how happy she was in her new home.

"Very well, Pollyanna," her aunt said one morning during a sewing lesson. "I'm glad your days are happy. But I trust that they are also profitable. Otherwise, I should have failed in my duty to you."

"But why must they be pro-fi-ta-ble?" asked the child. What does that word mean, anyhow?"

"It means having something to show for your

efforts."

"Then just being glad isn't enough?"

"Absolutely not!"

"Oh, dear. Now I'm afraid you'll never want to play the game, Aunt Polly!"

"Game? What game?"

"The one Father . . ."

She put her hand over her mouth, remembering that she wasn't supposed to talk about her father.

"Never mind," said Aunt Polly. "That's all for this morning." The sewing lesson was over.

That same afternoon, Pollyanna met her aunt in the attic.

"Aunt Polly, I'm so glad you're coming to see me—I just love company!"

Miss Polly, in fact, had not been planning to go to her niece's room, but rather to the garment bag to get a white shawl. To her great surprise, she found herself sitting on one of the straight-backed chairs in Pollyanna's bare little room. The child flitted back and forth be-

She Put Her Hand Over Her Mouth.

tween her bed and her windows.

"I love company!" Pollyanna repeated. "Specially since I have my very own room . . . I *do* like this room, even if it doesn't have carpets and curtains and pictures . . ."

"What's that?" her aunt scolded.

Pollyanna's face turned red.

"N-nothing. I truly didn't mean to say that, Aunt Polly."

"I guess not. But now that you've started, go ahead and finish."

"Well, I guess I've always wanted those things and I never had them. Once a rug came in the barrel and the Ladies Aid showed it to me, but it was torn and stained. And there was a picture once, but it was broken. I *do* love pretty things . . . but, honestly, Aunt Polly, I'm glad that there isn't a mirror because now I can't see my freckles . . ."

"That will do, Pollyanna!" declared Miss Polly, heading for the door. The white shawl was forgotten. The next day, Miss Polly or-

“I Love Company!”

dered Nancy to move Pollyanna's things to the room below the attic. Nancy ran to tell Pollyanna the good news.

"You're moving downstairs, miss! I bet you're glad about *that*! And I'm gonna put all your things there before your aunt gets a chance to change her mind!"

Pollyanna flew downstairs and dropped into her aunt's lap.

"Oh, thank you, Aunt Polly, for my new room! That room has *everything*—carpets, curtains, and *three* pictures, besides the picture outside the window! I'm *so* glad!"

"Very well, child. Just be sure to take proper care of everything. And, Pollyanna, do you know that you have banged two doors in this house just in the past half-minute!"

"Yes, I know. It's just that I was so happy I couldn't help it! Did you *ever* bang a door, Aunt Polly?"

"Well, I certainly hope not!"

"Oh, what a shame! That means that if you

"You're Moving Downstairs!"

were ever glad and felt like banging doors, you didn't bang them. Or else—maybe you were never glad about anything!"

“Maybe You Were Never Glad!”

She Thought of Him as The Man.

Chapter 9

The Man

During her walks around town, Pollyanna often met the Man. She thought of him as the Man because he seemed rather special. He usually wore a long black coat and a high silk hat. He had very pale skin, and grayish hair stuck out from his hat. He stood very straight and walked fast, never looking around in any direction. What Pollyanna noticed most, however, was that, except for his dog, he was always alone. She felt sorry for him.

"How do you do, sir?" she said to him one afternoon. "Isn't it a lovely day?"

The Man seemed startled.

"Did you speak to *me*?" he asked.

"Why, yes," smiled Pollyanna.

He walked on in silence. The next day when she saw him, Pollyanna called out, "It's not as lovely a day as yesterday, but it's still rather nice, don't you think?"

"Eh? Oh! Humph!" the Man grunted and walked quickly on his way. But the third time that Pollyanna greeted him, he stopped short.

"Listen here, child, who are you, and why do you speak to me everyday?"

"I'm Pollyanna Whittier, and I thought you looked lonesome. I'm so glad you stopped. Now we've met— only I don't know your name yet."

"Well, of all the . . ." muttered the Man, continuing to walk.

It was raining the next time Pollyanna saw the Man, but she greeted him with a bright smile.

"It isn't so nice today, is it?" she called out to him. "I'm glad it doesn't always rain!"

"Did You Speak to Me?" He Asked.

The Man didn't even grunt or turn his head this time. He quickened his stride, keeping his hands behind his back and his shoulders very straight. Pollyanna decided that he hadn't heard her. The next day, she spoke more loudly.

"Hello!" she chirped. "Aren't you glad it isn't yesterday? It's so lovely to see the sunshine again!"

The Man stopped and spun around toward her with a scowl on his face.

"Listen, little girl, let's settle something right now. I have other things than the weather to think about. I don't know whether the sun is shining or not!"

Pollyanna smiled brightly. "I didn't think you knew, sir. That's why I told you!"

"What?" The Man frowned. "Why don't you find somebody your own age to talk to?"

"I'd like to, sir, but there aren't many children around here. Still, it's all right. I like old folks too. I'm used to the Ladies' Aid . . ."

He Spun Around Toward Her.

"Humph! So I remind you of the Ladies' Aid? Indeed!"

Pollyanna laughed out loud.

"Oh, no, sir! You don't look a bit like a Ladies' Aider. And besides, I'm sure you're much nicer than you look!"

"Well, of all the . . ."

The next time Pollyanna met the Man, he stopped and said: "Good afternoon, Miss Whittier! Let me assure you that I *know* the sun is shining today!"

The Man always said "good morning" or "good afternoon" to Pollyanna after this. Even that brief greeting surprised Nancy, who was accompanying Pollyanna on her walk one day.

"Sakes alive, Miss Pollyanna! Did that man *speak* to *you*?"

"Yes, he always does—now."

"Do you know who he is?"

Pollyanna shook her head. She realized that the Man had never even told her his name.

"But he never speaks to *anyone!*" said

"I'm Sure You're Nicer Than You Look!"

Nancy, her eyes widening. "He's John Pendleton. He lives alone in the big house on Pendleton Hill. It's all very mysterious. He won't even hire a cook; he eats his meals at the hotel three times a day. I know a woman who waits on tables in the dining room there, and she told me that he always orders the cheapest things on the menu."

"It's hard to pay for your food when you're poor," said Pollyanna. "Father and I usually ate beans and fish balls. We used to say we were glad that we liked beans! Does Mr. Pendleton like beans, Nancy?"

"Who cares whether or not? Mr. Pendleton is the richest man in town! He could eat dollar bills if he wanted! He spends a lot of money traveling to foreign countries too."

"Well, he must give all his money to the church," Pollyanna said. "Maybe he's even a missionary!"

"Humph!" said Nancy. "But it sure is weird, him speakin' to you!"

"He Lives Alone in the Big House."

First, She Found a Kitten.

Chapter 10

Introducing Jimmy

August brought some new things into Pollyanna's life. First, she found a kitten on the street, looked all around the neighborhood for the family that it belonged to, and finally brought it home to Miss Polly.

"I'm really glad I didn't find its owner," she explained. "'Cause I just love kittens!"

Miss Polly hated cats even when they were clean and healthy—which this one clearly wasn't!

"Ugh!" she said. "What a filthy little beast! And I'm sure that it's sick and has fleas!"

"I know it! Poor little thing!" replied Pollyanna. "But I told everybody I talked to that I knew you would take it in—after all, you took *me* in when I was all alone and feeling sad!"

Miss Polly always felt helpless when she had to argue with Pollyanna. She sank back into her chair and threw up her hands. The same thing happened the following week, when her niece brought home a dog. Thus did the Harrington residence become home to two animals: Fluffy and Buffy.

When Pollyanna presented a ragged little boy, however, Miss Polly quickly took control of the situation.

Pollyanna had found the boy sitting in the grass, playing with a stick, alongside the road. Pollyanna was very glad to see someone about her own age. "Hello!" she said.

"Hello yourself!" he answered without raising his head.

"Well, you sure look like you could use some

She Threw Up Her Hands.

calf's-foot jelly!"

"Huh?" He looked up.

"Oh, never mind that! My name's Pollyanna Whittier. What's yours?"

"Jimmy Bean."

"Where do you live, Jimmy?"

"Nowhere."

"Nowhere? You can't mean that! Everybody lives *somewhere!*"

"Well, *I* don't! I'm lookin' for a new place."

"Where did you live before?"

"You sure ask a lot of questions!"

"I couldn't find out anything if I didn't!" she replied with a shrug.

Jimmy laughed half-heartedly.

"Well, then, here goes! I'm 10 years old—almost 11. I came to this town last year to live in the orphan house. But there's so many kids there already they hardly had room for me, and they didn't want me much anyway. So I'm huntin' for a new place . . . a regular home with a mother instead of a director. I have no folks

"Everybody Lives *Somewhere!*"

since Dad died. I already tried four houses. I even said I'd work, but none of them wanted me."

He glared at Pollyanna. "Is that all you want to know?"

"Oh, what a shame! I know just exactly how you feel. Nobody except the Ladies' Aid wanted me either after my father died. I was all alone and very unhappy. But then Aunt Polly . . ."

Suddenly a wonderful thought came to Pollyanna.

"I know just the place for you, Jimmy! I know my Aunt Polly will take you in to her house. She took Fluffy and Buffy when they had nobody to love them—and they're just cats and dogs!"

Jimmy's face brightened.

"Do you really think she'd take me? I can work hard!" he said, showing Pollyanna his arm muscles.

"Of course! Her house has *heaps* of rooms!

A Wonderful Thought Came to Pollyanna.

Maybe you'll have to sleep in the attic at first like I did. But it has screens now, so you can open the windows and the flies won't come in with their germs. Maybe Aunt Polly'll let you read about them if you're good—I mean, if you're bad. And you've got freckles too, so you'll be glad there's no mirror in the room . . ."

"How can you talk so fast?" Jimmy interrupted.

Pollyanna burst out laughing.

She told him to follow her home. Then Pollyanna ran into the room where her aunt sat reading.

"Oh, Aunt Polly! I've got such a nice surprise for you! He's so much nicer than Fluffy and Buffy! He's a real live boy for you to bring up! He can work too—but I reckon I'll need him most of the time to play with!"

Miss Polly's face turned white. She looked as if she might faint. Finally, she stammered:

"Pollyanna, what does this mean? Who is

Her Aunt Sat Reading.

this dirty little boy? Where did you find him?"

"Oh, I forgot to tell you his name! This is Jimmy Bean. And I know he's dirty, but Fluffy and Buffy were dirty too before I cleaned them up. I reckon Jimmy'll be fine as soon as he gets washed."

"BUT WHAT IS HE DOING HERE?"

"Why, I just told you!" said Pollyanna. "He's here to live with us! He wants a home and a family. I told him how good you are to me and Fluffy and Buffy, and I said you'd be good to him too!"

Miss Polly was beside herself!

"Pollyanna! It's bad enough you bring home dirty animals from the street. Now you've got a beggar . . ."

Jimmy walked forward.

"I'm no beggar, ma'am. I was thinkin' I'd work for you. And I wouldn't even be here 'cept this girl told me you'd be glad to take me in. So there!"

He turned and ran from the room and the

“I’m No Beggar, Ma’am.”

house as fast as his bony little legs could carry him.

"Why, Aunt Polly! I really did think you'd be *glad* to have Jimmy . . ."

"*Glad*!" spat Miss Polly. "*Will you please stop using that word*!" Polly clapped her hand over her mouth and raced outside to Jimmy.

"I'm *so* sorry!' she said.

"It isn't your fault," he answered. "I'll find a place."

"Maybe I can still help you!" Pollyanna said.

"How?"

"I'll talk to the Ladies' Aid. Father always went to them to teach the heathen or get a new carpet."

"Well, I'm no heathen or a carpet!" said Jimmy. "But what's a Ladies' Aid anyway?"

"It's just a bunch of ladies that meet and sew and give suppers and raise money and . . . I know one of them would give you a home!"

"You really think so? Be sure to tell them I can work," said the boy hopefully.

“Maybe I Can Still Help You!”

"I will. They meet this afternoon."

There was complete silence when Pollyanna entered the meeting room. Finally, Mrs. Ford, the minister's wife, asked:

"Did your aunt send you here?"

Pollyanna blushed.

"No," she admitted. "But I've known lots of Ladies' Aiders. They helped Father raise me . . ."

"Well, what can we do for you?" Mrs. Ford asked impatiently.

"Well, I came to talk to you about Jimmy Bean. He's only 10 years old, and he wants a home and family. He lives in the orphan house, but he wants a mother . . . and I thought one of you might let him live with you . . ."

Pollyanna stopped for breath.

"Well, did you ever?" one of the women started. Then the ladies began to chatter among themselves.

The problem seemed to be that the Ladies' Aid got "credit" in a certain report if they sent

"Did Your Aunt Send You Here?"

money to help children in India and other foreign countries where the church had missions. But there was no money—and no "credit"—to help little boys right in their own neighborhood.

Pollyanna couldn't find anything to be glad about in this situation. And how would she tell Jimmy?

There Was No Money.

He Was Barking Loudly and Running.

Chapter 11

On Pendleton Hill

On the way home, Pollyanna saw Mr. Pendleton's dog. Usually the animal was very calm and quiet, but today he was barking loudly and running between Pollyanna and the grassy area ahead. He seemed to be telling the little girl to follow him. But where was his master? Pollyanna soon found him. He was lying on the ground at the bottom of the hill.

"Mr. Pendleton! Are you hurt?"

"You don't think I'm lying here for the fun of it, do you?" he snapped and then quickly apologized. "Please forgive me. I've broken my leg."

He reached into his pocket and handed her some keys. "Could you go to my house and call Dr. Chilton? His name is on a card next to the phone. Ask him to come at once!"

"Oh, Mr. Pendleton! A broken leg! How awful! I'm so glad I came . . ."

"For heaven's sake, child! Can you stop talking and help me?" he pleaded.

Pollyanna ran to the house, called the doctor, and returned to Mr. Pendleton's side within minutes.

"I'm so glad I found him!" she told Dr. Chilton when he arrived.

"So am I," declared the doctor.

But her help for Mr. Pendleton made Pollyanna late for supper. She had to run all the way home.

"I sure am glad to see you! Where've you been?" cried Nancy.

Pollyanna told Nancy about her adventure on Pendleton Hill.

"Well, you're just lucky your aunt's gone so

"A Broken Leg! How Awful!"

she can't scold you!"

"Aunt Polly is *gone?*"

"Yes. Her cousin in Boston died, and she went to the funeral. I guess we should be glad that we'll be alone here at the house for the next few days."

"But Nancy, you can't be glad about a funeral! There must be some times when you can't play the game!"

When Miss Polly returned, her niece had a special favor to ask:

"Aunt Polly, would you mind very much if I took some calf's-foot jelly to a person who's not Mrs. Snow? Just this one time? He has a broken leg . . ."

"*He?* Broken leg? Pollyanna, what are you up to this time?" Miss Polly demanded.

"Oh, I forgot to tell you. But I found him lying on the ground, and he gave me the key to his house so I could call the doctor and . . ."

"Never mind, Pollyanna," said her aunt, who was very tired. "Take the jelly if you must. And

"Pollyanna, What Are You Up To?"

who did you say this man is?"

"Mr. John Pendleton."

Miss Polly fairly bolted from her chair.

"*John Pendleton!*"

"Yes, do you know him?"

"Do *you* know him, Pollyanna?"

"Oh, yes, Aunt Polly. He always speaks to me now. He looks mean, but he's really nice on the inside!"

She turned to go.

"Wait, Pollyanna!' called her aunt. "I changed my mind. I want you to give Mrs. Snow the jelly after all. I don't care to send jelly to Mr. Pendleton."

"But Aunt Polly! It will just be this one time! Broken legs get better. Mrs. Snow will be sick for a long time. And if you don't like Mr. Pendleton, I'll just tell him *I* sent the jelly, not you."

Miss Polly eyed her carefully. "Does he know you're my niece?"

"Oh, no, I never told him that."

"John Pendleton?"

"Very well, then. You may go to him with the jelly. But be sure that you don't say it's from me."

"Oh, thank you, Aunt Polly!" said the little girl with delight. She ran to the kitchen to get the jelly and raced out of the house— remembering not to bang the door behind her.

Remembering Not to Bang the Door

“Would You Like to See the Patient?”

Chapter 12

Dr. Chilton

"What have we here? Calf's-foot jelly!" said Dr. Chilton, opening the door to Mr. Pendleton's house. "Would you like to see the patient? Your cheerful face would help him more than a bottle of medicine!"

Pollyanna followed the doctor down a long hallway to Mr. Pendleton's room. The big mysterious house was no longer empty except for its owner. Not only was Dr. Chilton there, but a woman was in the kitchen cooking, another woman was dusting the furniture, and a nurse stood by with some medicines.

"Here's a visitor for you!" Dr. Chilton announced. The man in the bed frowned.

"Hello, sir. I brought you some calf's-foot jelly. I hope you like it," said Pollyanna.

"Never ate any of that stuff."

"Well, in that case, you can't know if you like it. So I reckon I'm glad I brought it for you to try!"

"What does it matter anyway if I'm flat on my back and likely to have to stay in bed 'til doomsday?"

"Oh, no, Mr. Pendleton! Not 'til doomsday! That's a very long time away! I know the Bible says it will come quicker than we think, but I really don't think so . . . "

Mr. Pendleton laughed suddenly.

"Anyway, maybe you should be glad you only broke one leg instead of two!" Pollyanna continued.

"Yes, and if I was a centipede—an insect with 50 legs—I might have broken them all!" he answered.

"Not 'Til Doomsday!"

"That's right!" said Pollyanna, clapping her hands. "I think you're learning to play the game, sir!"

"Who cares about games?" Mr. Pendleton said crossly. "Here I've got all these people in my way trying to clean up my house and cook my meals, and they want me to pay them good money!"

"Oh, yes, the money," said Pollyanna, remembering her conversation with Nancy. "Nancy told me you save all your money for the heathen. That's how I know you're good inside even when you're mean on the outside."

"What on earth are you talking about, child? And who is Nancy?"

"She works for Aunt Polly."

"And who, may I ask, is Aunt Polly?"

"She's Miss Polly Harrington. I live with her."

Mr. Pendleton turned as white as a ghost and sat upright in bed, moaning in pain with the sudden movement of his broken leg.

"Who Cares About Games?"

"You live with—*her*?"

She nodded.

"But you don't mean that *she* sent me this jelly!"

"No, sir. She said I must be sure not to let you think that she sent it. But . . ."

"I thought so," he answered bitterly. His expression frightened Pollyanna. She decided it was time to leave. Outside, Dr. Chilton was waiting with his horse and carriage to drive her home.

"Thank you!" she beamed. "I just love to ride!"

"Seems there's lot of things you love to do!" he responded.

"Most of all, I love to *live*! said Pollyanna. "All those other things I have to do—sewing, reading out loud, cooking—they're not really living. Aunt Polly says they are 'learning to live.' But tell me, why do people have to *learn* to live?"

"I'm afraid some of us have to," the doctor

"I Just Love to Ride!"

sighed. He appeared sad.

"Dr. Chilton, you must have the gladdest job in the world!" said Pollyanna, trying to cheer him up.

"Gladdest? I see so much suffering among my patients!"

"But you're *helping* people!" she insisted. "That's something to be *very* glad about!"

Thomas Chilton regarded his work simply as a way to keep busy and escape from his lonely life. Now he thought about Pollyanna's words.

"Who was that man who drove you home?" asked Miss Polly as soon as her niece entered the house.

"That was Dr. Chilton. Don't you know him?"

"Dr. Chilton—he came *here?*" Miss Polly stiffened.

"Oh, and I told Mr. Pendleton that you didn't send him the jelly."

A look of anger flashed over her aunt's face.

“Dr. Chilton Came *Here*?”

"You *told* him I didn't?"

"That's what you told me to do, Aunt Polly!"

"I told you not to let him think I *did* send it. That's not the same thing as telling him I *didn't* send it," she explained. But Pollyanna couldn't understand the difference.

The little girl also couldn't understand why her aunt never tried to look pretty. She had beautiful black curly hair but always wore it pinned back tightly. She also wore very plain clothes and never put on jewelry or any other ornaments.

"Please, Aunt Polly," she begged one day, "let me do your hair just like I did Mrs. Snow's! Just sit right down here in front of the dressing table."

"Pollyanna, this is silly . . ." her aunt began, but then she got the helpless feeling that this amazing child always gave her.

"Now I want to be sure you don't peek in the mirror yet," said Pollyanna after she arranged the curls. Before her aunt could protest, she

"Please Let Me Do Your Hair!"

tied a handkerchief around her eyes.

"Take this thing off me! What *are* you doing?" said Miss Polly frantically.

Pollyanna slipped a white lace shawl around her aunt's shoulders. Then she picked a red rose out of a nearby vase and put it gently in Miss Polly's hair.

"There!" she exclaimed, removing the handkerchief.

Instead of looking in the mirror, Miss Polly stared at the window and then ran out of the room, pulling the shawl off and tossing the flower from her hair. Flushed and angry, she demanded, "How could you let this happen, Pollyanna? You dressed me up like this and then let me be seen!"

Pollyanna saw Dr. Chilton's carriage in the driveway. She hurried outside.

"Mr. Pendleton wants to see you," he said. "Can you come?"

"Yes, and I reckon Aunt Polly will be glad to get rid of me!"

A White Shawl

The doctor looked surprised.

"Didn't I just see you with your aunt through the window?"

"Yes. I fixed her hair. Don't you think she looked really pretty?"

"Yes, she *did* look lovely."

"I'm so glad you agree. I can't wait to tell her!"

"No, Pollyanna! Don't do that!"

They drove the rest of the way in silence.

"Didn't I Just See Your Aunt?"

He Showed Pollyanna His Books.

Chapter 13

A Mystery Solved?

"It was nice of you to come," Mr. Pendleton greeted her. "I'm sorry I was so cross the last time. I didn't thank you for helping me when I fell—or for the jelly."

He showed Pollyanna his books and the wonderful things he had brought home from his travels all over the world. Then he said:

"I hope you'll come here often. I'm lonesome and I need your company. There's another reason too."

"What is that?" asked Pollyanna.

"Well, you remind me of something that I've

tried to forget but now I want to remember again. Will *you* come again, Pollyanna?"

"Yes, I'd love to!" she beamed.

When she got home, Pollyanna told Nancy about the conversation.

"And he said you reminded him of something he had wanted to forget?" Nancy questioned her. "What was it?"

"He didn't say."

"It sure is a mystery," said Nancy. "But I think I can solve it!"

"You can?"

"Yes! Wasn't it right after Mr. Pendleton found out that you were Miss Polly's niece that he said he never wanted to see you again? And didn't you also tell him that Miss Polly didn't send the jelly?"

"Well, yes . . . And he *did* start sounding strange after that . . ." Pollyanna recalled.

"That's it for sure!" declared Nancy. "*Mr. Pendleton was Miss Polly Harrington's sweetheart!*"

"It Sure Is a Mystery," Said Nancy.

Nancy grinned from ear to ear. "Listen, Miss Pollyanna. Just before you came to live here, Mr. Tom told me Miss Polly used to have a sweetheart and he was still right in this town. It's got to be Mr. Pendleton! He lives all alone in that big house and never talks to a soul. And he told you that you remind him of something he wanted to forget. Imagine them bein' sweethearts!"

"But it's impossible, Nancy! She doesn't even like him!" Pollyanna protested.

"Of course not, they quarreled."

"But wouldn't they be glad to make up?" asked the little girl.

"I'm afraid you don't know too much about sweethearts, Miss Pollyanna. There ain't two people in the world less willin' to play your 'glad' game than two quarrelin' sweethearts!"

Nancy chuckled.

"But you know, Miss Pollyanna, it sure would be somethin' if you could get them to play that game!"

"Miss Polly Used to Have a Sweetheart."

Pollyanna noticed that her aunt seemed to dislike Dr. Chilton even more than she did Mr. Pendleton. Miss Polly refused to call him when the little girl got a bad cold.

"Dr. Chilton is *not* our family doctor!" Miss Polly declared. "Dr. Warren will take care of you."

Pollyanna wondered why.

“Dr. Warren Will Take Care of You.”

Boys and Girls Her Own Age

Chapter 14

Secrets

Pollyanna entered school in September. Finally she was able to meet lots of boys and girls her own age. But she still tried to find time for her older friends, especially Mr. Pendleton.

"I miss you, Pollyanna," he told her one day. "I don't see nearly enough of you now that you go to school. How would you like to come and live with me?"

"You know I can't, Mr. Pendleton. I'm—Aunt Polly's!"

His face became very sad, and he spoke

gently.

"Many years ago, Pollyanna, I loved someone very much. I wanted to bring her to this house and to have a family. It didn't happen, and I've been all alone ever since. This house has never really been a home. Only a woman's hand and heart or a child's presence can make it a home. That's why I want you to live here."

"Oh, Mr. Pendleton! Do you . . . mean that you wish you . . . had that woman's hand and heart all this time?" Pollyanna whispered.

"Well, y . . . yes, Pollyanna."

"It's all settled then!" chirped the little girl. "I'm so glad! You can take us both! If you just tell Aunt Polly everything like you told me, I'm sure she'll want to come!"

"*You want your Aunt Polly to come here?*"

"We could all live at her house if you'd like that better . . ." Pollyanna began.

Mr. Pendleton moaned. "Pollyanna, I beg you, please don't tell your aunt about anything we talked about!"

"You Want Your Aunt Polly to Come Here?"

"Of course, Mr. Pendleton. I know you want to tell her yourself!"

Pollyanna explained to Dr. Chilton on the way home that she hadn't meant to upset Mr. Pendleton.

"Anyway, it was Aunt Polly, not me, that upset him," she stated.

"What do you mean?"

"Well, he told me not to say anything to her, and I guess he wants to tell her himself like sweethearts do."

"Sweethearts?"

The doctor stopped the carriage with a jerk.

"It's a lovely story," smiled Pollyanna. "And I didn't even know it 'til Nancy told me that Aunt Polly used to have a sweetheart and they quarreled. She didn't know who it was at first. But now we found out that it was Mr. Pendleton!"

Dr. Chilton relaxed his hands on the reins and turned to Pollyanna.

"Mr. Pendleton wants to see you tomorrow," he said. "It's extremely important!"

"It's Extremely Important!"

John Pendleton was very nervous when Pollyanna arrived the next day.

"I've been trying to figure out what you meant about my wanting your aunt's hand and heart," he told her.

"Why, because you were sweethearts once and I was so glad you still felt that way about Aunt Polly!"

"*Miss Polly and I? Sweethearts?*"

"Do you mean . . . it isn't true?" asked the child. There was deep disappointment in her voice. "And it would have been so lovely for both of us to come here to live with you."

"Won't you come by yourself?"

"Oh, I can't do that, sir! I belong to Aunt Polly!"

John Pendleton stared at her.

"Before you were hers, Pollyanna, you were . . . your mother's. And it was your mother's hand and heart that I wanted for so long!"

"*My mother's!*" Pollyanna could not believe her ears!

"I Belong to Aunt Polly!"

"I loved your mother, but she didn't love me, and after a while she went away with . . . your father. My whole world just fell apart."

Pollyanna's eyes filled with tears as she listened.

"When you came into my life with your cheer—your *gladness*—at first I never wanted to see you again because you reminded me of your mother. But now I want to see you all the time!"

"But I can't just leave Aunt Polly!" she protested.

"What about *me*, Pollyanna? It's only since I met you that I've been glad to live. If you were my own little girl, I could be glad all the time. And we could play your glad game together!"

His voice softened and he looked sadly out the window.

"But Aunt Polly has been so good to me. She's glad to have me."

"Glad!" he answered sharply. "Your aunt doesn't know *how* to be glad. She always does

"My Whole World Fell Apart."

her duty, but she isn't the 'glad' type."

"Well, anyway, I'm glad I didn't tell Aunt Polly what you told me yesterday. I only told Dr. Chilton."

"You told the doctor?"

Mr. Pendleton bolted upright, moaning in pain. Pollyanna wondered if his broken leg hurt or if it could be that something else was bothering him.

“I Only Told the Doctor.”

Nancy Met Her with an Umbrella.

Chapter 15

A Change Of Heart

It was raining when Pollyanna started home. Nancy met her halfway with an umbrella.

"Miss Polly sure was worried about you. I said *worried.*"

"Oh, I'm sorry," replied the child. "I didn't mean to scare her."

"But you don't understand!" Nancy insisted. "Bein' worried means she's gettin' to be human—not just doin' her duty."

"Well, I'm glad you said that, because I was going to ask you if you think Aunt Polly likes to have me, and would she mind if I went away?"

Nancy had always feared that Pollyanna would want to leave. But now she could reassure her.

"Would your aunt send me here with this umbrella if she didn't care about you, Miss Pollyanna? She's really softenin' up!"

"Oh, Nancy! I'm so glad that Aunt Polly really wants me!"

It wasn't easy to tell John Pendleton.

"I've thought of the very gladdest thing you could do!" she said when she saw him the next day.

"With you, Pollyanna."

"Well . . . no . . . but . . ."

"Then your aunt wouldn't let you come to live with me?"

"I didn't ask her!"

"Pollyanna!" he declared.

"I couldn't," she explained. "I found out that Aunt Polly really *does* want me to stay with

"She's Really Softenin' Up!"

her. But let me tell you about the gladdest thing there is! All that money you save for the heathen . . ."

"Stop that nonsense, Pollyanna! I've never given them one penny!"

"Well, I'm glad about that," she replied. "Not about the heathen, of course. But I'm glad you don't give money to boys in India, because now you can take Jimmy Bean!" She told him Jimmy's story. "He'd be a perfect child's presence for you!"

"You Can Take Jimmy Bean!"

To Go to Dr. Chilton's Office

Chapter 16

An Accident

One day after school, Pollyanna stopped at Dr. Chilton's office to pick up some medicine for Mrs. Snow. Even though she was very busy with schoolwork and her other activities, she always made time to visit the sick woman. They became fast friends. Pollyanna's visits were the happiest times of Mrs. Snow's life—perhaps the *only* happy times. During her latest visit, the child had offered to go get the medicine from Dr. Chilton's office.

"What a nice place!" said Pollyanna when she arrived at the doctor's.

"Oh well, it's just some rooms—not really a home," he replied.

"I know. Mr. Pendleton said it takes a woman's hand and heart or a child's presence to make a real home."

Dr. Chilton laughed strangely.

"Oh, and I forgot to tell you that it wasn't Aunt Polly that Mr. Pendleton used to love, so we're not going to live at his house. But why don't *you* find a woman's hand and heart, Dr. Chilton?"

The doctor's face had a painful expression. "My dear Pollyanna, such things are not always there for the asking," he said quietly.

Pollyanna's eyes grew wide.

"Do you mean you tried to get somebody's hand and heart once, like Mr. Pendleton did, and you couldn't?"

The doctor, not answering, gave her the medicine for Mrs. Snow. Pollyanna left his office but couldn't help wondering about the secrets in the doctor's life. Dr. Chilton, Aunt

"Why Don't *You* Find a Woman's Heart?"

Polly, and Mr. Pendleton all lived by themselves, and all of them seemed very unhappy. Pollyanna wished she could cheer them up.

Pollyanna crossed the street to Mrs. Snow's house. From out of nowhere, a speeding car suddenly knocked her down. She lost consciousness. A stranger picked up her limp body and carried it to Miss Polly's house. Pollyanna did not know what had happened to her until she awoke many days later.

Miss Polly was at her bedside, holding her hand and trying not to cry.

"What's the matter, Aunt Polly? Is it time to get up?" the child asked.

Pollyanna tried to lift herself and fell back against the pillow.

"I *can't* get up, Aunt Polly! Why can't I get up?"

"Rest now, dear," her aunt replied gently. "A car hurt you. Just stay in bed for a while and you'll get better."

"But, Aunt Polly, my legs feel so funny! I

From Out of Nowhere

mean, I don't *feel* them at all!"

Miss Polly could find no words to ease her niece's fright.

"I guess I'm not glad to be hurt," Pollyanna said, trying to smile. "But I'm glad it's just my legs, like Mr. Pendleton, and not everything, like Mrs. Snow."

At that moment, Nancy was downstairs escorting John Pendleton, on crutches, into the sun parlor.

"Can you believe that John Pendleton has come to this house?" Nancy ran to tell Old Tom in the garden.

"They hardly talked for years!" the gardener replied. "After Miss Jenny went off to marry that minister chap, Miss Polly felt sorry for Mr. Pendleton and tried to be nice to him. But then folks around town began sayin' that she was chasin' him. She got so upset she never spoke to him again!"

Nancy listened with wide eyes.

"Then came Miss Polly's trouble with her

“I’m Not Glad to Be Hurt.”

own sweetheart," Old Tom continued. "After that, she didn't want to see anybody at all. She just shut herself up in this house, and her heart turned cold as ice!"

Mr. Pendleton greeted Miss Polly stiffly.

"I just came to find out how Pollyanna is," he said.

"No one knows," she replied. "Not even Dr. Warren."

"But what kind of injuries does she have? Do you know?"

"Some slight cuts and bruises—and an injury to the spine that paralyzed her from the hips down."

There were tears in Miss Polly's eyes and her voice shook.

"I should tell you," said Mr. Pendleton, "that I wanted Pollyanna to live with me. I wanted to adopt her. I am very fond of that little girl, both for her own sake and for her mother's. But she wouldn't come with me. She said that you were very good to her and she didn't want

Mr. Pendleton Greeted Miss Polly Stiffly.

to leave you."

Miss Polly listened carefully. Suddenly she realized that she had almost lost Pollyanna twice: once to John Pendleton and once to the car that had almost killed her.

She Almost Lost Pollyanna Twice.

"I Do Want to See Dr. Chilton!"

Chapter 17

A Waiting Game

"Pollyanna, another doctor is going to see you to try to help you get well faster," said Miss Polly several days later.

"Oh, Aunt Polly! I *do* want to see Dr. Chilton! I was afraid you wouldn't let him come . . ."

"I'm not talking about Dr. Chilton, dear," her aunt replied gently. "This is a very famous doctor from New York. He knows all about injuries like the one you have."

"But he can't know more than Dr. Chilton!" Pollyanna protested. "Dr. Chilton took care of Mr. Pendleton's broken leg, and it's almost better. Please let Dr. Chilton come to help me, Aunt Polly!"

Miss Polly looked closely at her niece.

"Pollyanna, please believe that I would do almost anything for you, but for reasons that I can't explain to you, I cannot allow Dr. Chilton to come here."

"But I love Dr. Chilton!" Pollyanna exclaimed. "And if *you* loved him instead of that other man—"

"It's all settled, Pollyanna," interrupted Miss Polly. " The doctor from New York will be here tomorrow."

Dr. Mead arrived right on time. He was attractive, well dressed, and friendly. After examining Pollyanna, he left her room and went out into the hall to confer with Miss Polly, Dr. Warren, and the nurse. If Fluffy the cat hadn't pushed the door open with her paw, Pollyanna would not have heard Aunt Polly's terrible cry:

"Doctor! You can't mean that the child will never walk again!" Then Miss Polly fainted

Dr. Mead Arrived Right on Time.

dead away.

"Aunt Polly! Aunt Polly!" the terrified little girl screamed from her bed. "Please come here!"

The nurse entered.

"Your aunt can't come now. Just wait a few minutes . . ."

"But I want her *now*! I heard her say something terrible, and I want her to tell me it isn't true!"

The look on the nurse's face said that it *was* true.

"You heard the doctor!" cried Pollyanna. And it *is* true, isn't it? I'll never be able to walk again!"

"Maybe he doesn't know for sure," said the nurse weakly. "Maybe he made a mistake."

"But Aunt Polly said he knows more than any other doctor about broken legs like mine!"

"Try to get some sleep, dear," said the nurse, handing Pollyanna the little white pills.

"But I don't want to sleep! I want to go to

"Aunt Polly! Aunt Polly!"

school and to Mr. Pendleton's house and to Mrs. Snow's!" Pollyanna sobbed. And suddenly, she said in terror, "If I can't walk, how am I ever going to be glad for *anything?*"

"How Can I Be Glad for Anything?"

"That Poor Little Girl!"

Chapter 18

The Game and Its Players

Miss Polly sent Nancy to give John Pendleton the bad news about Pollyanna. She had promised to let him know what the new doctor said.

"That poor little girl! Never to dance in the sunshine again! Never to give her cheerful greeting to people along the streets! Never to bring joy to them in their homes! It is so cruel and unfair!"

"Not only that," Nancy added. "She's worried because it'll be so hard to play the 'glad' game. Do you know about that?"

He nodded.

"Well, I reminded her that she said it was nicer to play the game when it was hard—but she said that now it's *really* hard!"

Not long afterword, Mr. Pendleton stopped by. His broken leg was all better, and the crutches were gone.

"Please give Pollyanna a very important message for me," he begged Miss Polly. "Tell her that I've decided to bring Jimmy Bean to live with me. I shall probably adopt him as my own little boy."

Miss Polly dutifully delivered the message to her niece. Pollyanna clapped her hands, and her face brightened up for the first time since the accident.

"I'm *so* glad!" she exclaimed. "Now Mr. Pendleton and Jimmy will both have a real home!"

Everyone in the town seemed to have met Pollyanna—even people who were not acquainted with Miss Polly Harrington. And

A Very Important Message

everyone seemed to remember a time when Pollyanna had taught them how to be glad about something. They came to Miss Polly's house, one after the other, and talked about playing the "glad" game. Miss Polly was indeed puzzled. She went to see Nancy in the kitchen and demanded an explanation of these strange happenings.

"Everybody in this town is wearing blue ribbons, stopping family quarrels, being nice to less fortunate people, giving more money to charity, or starting to like something they never liked before—and it's all because of Pollyanna. And they keep babbling about some game. Will you *please* let me know what's going on?"

"Miss Pollyanna tried to tell you about the game, but you wouldn't let her talk about her father, and he's the one that taught her to play it."

"Never mind that, Nancy. Just explain it to me."

"It's All Because of Pollyanna."

"Very well, ma'am. Once Miss Pollyanna told the Ladies Aid that she hoped there would be a doll in the next barrel of things they collected. But when the barrel arrived, there was no doll. All she got was a pair of crutches. So she cried, as any child would. But her father told her that there was always somethin' about everything that you could be glad about and that she should be glad about the crutches."

Miss Polly thought about Pollyanna's helpless little legs on the bed upstairs.

"He told her to be glad because she didn't *need* the crutches," Nancy continued. "And she listened carefully and began to agree with him. Pollyanna has been playin' the 'glad' game ever since! And she wants everybody to play it with her."

"Well, I know somebody who's going to play it now!" declared Miss Polly, rushing to her niece's room.

"Everybody in this town is happier since you

"Pollyanna's Been Playin' the 'Glad Game'."

came, Pollyanna, and it's all because of your game!"

"Well, then I'm glad that I *used to have* my legs so that I was able to meet them!" beamed the little girl, clapping her hands with joy.

"It's All Because of Your Game!"

He Couldn't Keep His Mind Off Pollyanna.

Chapter 19

A New Uncle

The winter passed slowly. Pollyanna missed school and was eager to see the many friends she had made there. She passed much of the time knitting bright-colored things and being glad, like Mrs. Snow, that she had her arms and hands even though her legs didn't work.

Dr. Chilton could not keep his mind off Pollyanna. He was very fond of the little girl and could not bear to think of her suffering.

"I *must* examine that child!" he told John

Pendleton a few months after the accident. "But Miss Polly Harrington once told me that if she ever let me into her house again, it would mean that she wanted to be forgiven and to marry me."

"But why can't you go without waiting for an invitation?"

"I *do* have some professional pride," said the doctor. "I can't just offer my advice when it isn't asked for. But I *do* believe that Pollyanna can walk again! I hate to see my old quarrel with her aunt get in the way!"

Mr. Pendleton listened closely.

"Pollyanna's case sounds like one that a friend of mine treated," Dr. Chilton said. "This is his special field of study. Now *I must find a way to see that little girl!*"

"How can we make it happen?" asked Mr. Pendleton.

"Darned if I know!"

"Well, by jinx, *I* know!" thought Jimmy Bean, who was working in the garden outside

"Well, By Jinx, *I* Know!"

Mr. Pendleton's house and heard the conversation through the window. He raced to the Harrington house and begged Nancy to let him see Miss Polly.

"I want to see you because of Pollyanna," he spoke up bravely. "When I tell you it's only pride—or something like that—that's keepin' Pollyanna from maybe walkin' again, maybe you'll let Dr. Chilton come . . ."

"What are you saying?" Miss Polly fairly shouted with anger. "How dare you come here and speak to me like this!"

"I didn't want to make you angry, ma'am, but if it means Pollyanna walking again . . ."

"Now tell me exactly what you *do* mean," Miss Polly said more gently.

"Well, Dr. Chilton came to see Mr. Pendleton, and they were talkin' in the library and the window was open, and I was workin' outside in the garden and I couldn't help but hear . . ."

"Very well, Jimmy. Go on."

He Spoke Up Bravely.

"Well, ma'am, Dr. Chilton knows some doctor somewhere that maybe can help Pollyanna walk, but he wants to see her before he calls that doctor. And he says he can't see her because you wouldn't let him in."

"But, Jimmy! I. . . .can't! I explained to Pollyanna that I can't allow Dr. Chilton to come here."

"I hope you change your mind, ma'am," he replied, "because it sure would mean a lot to Pollyanna!"

As soon as the boy left, Miss Polly instructed Dr. Warren to call Dr. Chilton in to discuss Pollyanna's case. He arrived that same day.

"Pollyanna, today you have done one of the gladdest things in your whole life!" Dr. Chilton greeted her when he came into her room.

That evening, a new Aunt Polly, soft, gentle, and beaming with happiness, came to sit on the edge of the little girl's bed and said, "Next

He Arrived that Same Day.

week you're going to take a trip to see a famous doctor, a friend of Dr. Chilton's, who will try to make your legs better."

Then she gave her niece a very surprising piece of news.

"Pollyanna, you are the first to know. I'm going to give Dr. Chilton to you for your uncle! And you made it happen! I'm so happy—so *glad!*"

Miss Polly and Nancy helped Pollyanna pack her things for the trip to the doctor. The big house seemed quiet and empty when she was gone, but Pollyanna's letter a month later brought good news:

"Dear Aunt Polly and Uncle Tom:

"Oh, I can—I can—I *can* walk! I did today all the way from my bed to the window! It was six steps. My, how good it was to be on legs again!

"All the doctors stood around and smiled, and all the nurses stood beside of them and cried. A lady in the next ward who walked

"Pollyanna, You Are the First to Know."

last week first, peeked into the door, and another one who hopes she can walk next month, was invited in to the party, and she laid on my nurse's bed and clapped her hands. Even Tilly, who washes the floor, looked through the window and called me, 'Honey child' when she wasn't crying too much to call me anything.

"I don't see why they cried. *I* wanted to sing and shout and yell! Oh—oh—oh! Just think, I can walk—walk—*walk!* Now I don't mind being here almost ten months, and I didn't miss the wedding, anyhow. Wasn't that just like you, Aunt Polly, to come here and get married right beside my bed, so I could see you. You always do think of the gladdest things!

"Pretty soon, they say, I shall go home. I wish I could walk all the way there. I do. I don't think I shall ever want to ride anywhere any more. It will be so good just to walk. Oh, I'm so glad! I'm glad for every-

"I Can Walk—Walk—*Walk*!"

thing. Why, I'm glad now I lost my legs for a while, for you never, never know how perfectly lovely legs are till you haven't got them—legs that go, I mean. I'm going to walk eight steps to-morrow.

"With heaps of love to everybody,

Pollyanna."

“With Heaps of Love to Everybody, Pollyanna.”

Made in the USA
Coppell, TX
25 January 2022

72300136R00134